Purepero Stories

Maria del Carmen Cortez and
Rebekah Eppley

Artwork by Juan Luis Cortez and Maria
del Carmen Cortez

Nomadic Press
2017

This book was made possible by a loving community of family and friends, old and new.

Requests for permission to make copies of any part of the work should be sent to
info@nomadicpress.org.

For author questions or to book a reading at your school, bookstore, or alternative
establishment, please send an email to info@nomadicpress.org.

Published by Nomadic Press, 2926 Foothill Boulevard, Oakland, California, 94601
www.nomadicpress.org

First Edition
First Printing

Library of Congress Cataloging-in-Publication Data

Cortez, Maria del Carmen, and Eppley, Rebekah, 1966 – and 1965 – , respectively
Purepero Stories/written by Maria del Carmen Cortez and Rebekah Eppley; artwork by
Juan Luis Cortez and Maria del Carmen Cortez; illustrated by Arthur Johnstone
p. cm.
Summary: A collaborative project told in words and images, *Purepero Stories* captures
the life of a young Mexican girl growing up in Mexico and California with her sisters, tia
Rosa, and grandmothers. The stories are told by a Michoacana and seasonal immigrant to
California to her new romantic partner as a way of introducing her culture and heritage.
Myths, history, and truth blend as the stories unravel to reveal a life between cultures.
[1. FICTION / Subjects & Themes / Family; 2. FICTION / Subjects & Themes / History;
3. FICTION / American / General.] I. Title.

2017956263

ISBN: 978-0-9994471-3-0

The illustrations in this book were created using watercolor and ink on Canson paper.
The type was set in Garamond Premier Pro.
Printed and bound in the United States
Typesetting and book design by J. K. Fowler
Edited by Ari Moskowitz and J. K. Fowler

In loving memory of
Juan Luis Cortez

CONTENTS

WHERE WE MEET

There's a burro in my Vermont winter, a rebozo in my October turning leaves, a sombrero in slow summer, spring we've yet to know. There's a lumberjack in your back patio, no rhythm in my carnival, a chill in San Isidro, still saints for other days. These words, the last leaves spiral down, landing on my sled, my hills of snow, my frozen icicle feet, my salty, your sweet, your warm nights of ghosts and buried gold, ripe fruit at harvest, your stories in volcanoes and sleepy mountain slopes. Words exploding where breasts form against clouds, whose hills a secret passage gaining entry. And on the other side this night we stand still for a moment, look up and remember in stars.

BEGINNINGS

In your childhood home we gather around the table with your sisters. Your mother serves eggs and fresh tortillas with queso, sets a small pail of milk on the table before us. We keep our bodies contained, hold back the touch between us and focus on your sisters and their families, trying to find the space where we fit. Spanish flows through your lips, your language of familiar. I gather bits and pieces, a slow translation but there's enough of you within the words so that I understand.

In the corral you name fruit trees, point out the pens where the animals were kept, the wall where you slipped and chipped a tooth, the spot outside the kitchen window where you and your sisters once saw a ghost. Memories of buried gold, bloody slaughters, the sweetness of fruit, all held within the same history.

Later that day, walking in the plaza, you tell me your desire was always to be among your friends rather than seeking the affection of boys. Now we sit on a bench watching young women walk circles around the kiosk, each one waiting for a man to make the first move.

At night in your childhood bedroom we relax into our familiar touch, our bodies at rest. Rain slides off teja rooftops, soothing us into sleep. My own country childhood lies far off in the States and yet I remember the stillness of night, the animal smells, hay in the fields.

The next day we walk through town. An old woman sits on a bench, dressed in a long, pleated skirt, a rebozo wrapped around her shoulders. She looks like your abuelita Herminia you tell me, a woman who honors Purepecha traditions. We're walking arm in arm, a custom for two women here, when the woman looks at us and speaks through her gaze, a welcome recognition. It's nothing mystical, no billowing clouds of smoke, just an ordinary moment filled with knowing. She winks, nods her head as a slow grin spreads, her body illuminated, as if she sees all. We walk on, hold our silence, the three of us briefly linked before you and I look at one another, mouthing the words "What was that?" because we aren't really sure we've seen her. It's our gem, our sole souvenir — the connection in being seen.

Back at the house we lie in bed, restless. We've planned a trip into the mountains for tomorrow and already you're flooded with stories.

All your memories, myths and truths blend and meld, leading us into this new journey, leading us to we don't know where.

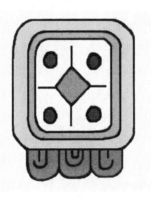

GLIMPSES

On the ride to your mother's village, dust rises from the dirt road and slowly settles over your clothes, forming a third layer like protection. You look to the hills and patches of red-brown earth matched to the tone of your skin.

Leaning against the rickety railings of the open bed truck, you brace your body against twists and turns, trusting the old farmer who guides us through these lonely roads.

Already you've drifted into your world, remembering cherry trees and pines slanted against the wind, the solitary oaks and deep maroon of the madrone smooth against your hands and family gatherings in the mountains with Christmas piñatas and crackling, sparkling lights. You remember this same trip many years ago and the excitement of sleeping in new beds and waking in crisp mountain air with your tias, recognizing your mother in all their faces.

Now you arrive in silence to a town abandoned, a dusty landscape carried on whispering winds. Tia, you call to a face in the window who fades as the word leaves your lips. Through the doors she emerges with arms outstretched, a fine rain of cornmeal sprinkled over her clothes. You reach for her hands and hold the fingers, calloused and blistered, tight in your own. Life here is still what you make with your hands. You feel for the life in those hands that carved for you a smoother future.

Further up the mountain road sits the house where your mother was born, where her siblings still live. The young ones, they say, moved to the cities. They don't want this life anymore. And while you don't blame them, you long for a piece of it still.

The house embraces the girl your mother once was, the child you were, and the stories that passed through the night. A stone basin catches rainwater for washing. Colorful birds in hanging cages blend songs with those flying free. You see your mother in flowers and night blooming jasmine. You smell her in bitter anise and sweet cacao. Searching for history just out of reach, you grasp for the shape of her past.

PIÑATA STORIES

You remember Rosa on her chair on the stoop. She watches and rocks while in the street you and your friends push one another toward a bright colored star hanging luminous just out of reach. Each crack of the stick tempts you with treats. Tamarindo dulces and smooth tejocotes hidden deep within like a sweet secret wish.

Rosa sits on the stoop with those who are left. Sisters and friends mapping time on their faces, deep creases of rivers and valleys embedded in the flesh. Together they are their own stories, words and fragments held in memory, close to bursting.

On the road each child twists and spins, turns a reckless dance with fast flowing limbs. You will be different you think as you reach for the stick and grab a firm hold. With eyes sealed shut behind the blindfold you give in to the spin. Your body feels weightless as your feet find direction. Through measured swings you keep your aim exact and stand in the dark beneath a sudden explosion as treasures spill down your arms and drop to the ground. Voices blend as the others rush beside you beneath the bright bursting star. You don't worry about missing the candies and sweets now freely scattered about your feet. Just knowing you were the one who broke through is enough; it was you who fed the greedy voices.

On the stoop, Rosa watches and waits for the day when you will need stories to feed you, when her words will spill freely and scatter across the landscape, landing at your feet and you will stand in amazement once again and close your eyes, content just to listen.

THE HEADLESS PRIEST

Listen, Rosa whispered. *When you're quiet enough, who knows what you'll hear.* When your parents worked in the States, Great Aunt Rosa came to your house with her words, covering adobe walls in shadow and coloring your nights with hauntings. You and your sisters squeezed into bed while Rosa spun tales through the night and left you your history, her voice hushed and mysterious as you huddled together in delighted fear while Rosa smiled and let you believe in a world beyond your familiar.

Not far from here, was always the beginning, where the twin ranches road winds into the hills. Rosa told of the priest who camped at the ranches, resting after his journey on horseback from city to country, scattering his teachings among trees and grass, sky and deep-red earth. While he slept, stars hung bright behind a silver moon washed in silence.

Gunshots burst through the night, but he didn't hear a sound, the bullets passing through his body so quickly he had no time to feel, Rosa whispers, her voice so low you lean in close to catch the words. The next day herders made their way into the hills and found the priest lying next to the ranch. His head was severed from his body, the horse lying on its side with chains tangled about its neck and flank.

Those nights with Aunt Rosa, you and your sisters heard them, the horse dragging its chains, the headless priest at the reins restless in death and searching. You'd lie in bed, seven tiny girls nestled together with eyes wide open, resisting sleep while he passed by your window, reminding you that nothing is too holy, nothing too sacred. Seven heads quickly disappeared beneath the blankets as you muffled your shrieks, each of you learning rituals and chants carried far into other nights.

CROSSING THE BORDER

You were seven the first time you came to the States with your family looking for work. Every spring after that you followed the same route, the station wagon filled with eight girls in the back, restless and anxious for the three-day journey to end. The trip lingered on in dreams and sleepy awakenings, landscapes etched into memory. The shapes of women stretched across mountain slopes in Michoacan. Jalisco lay in lava fields, rocks and dirt scattered into random formation. Rich, green jungles covered Nayarit. Sinaloa was endless brown desert, blending into Sonora and then finally La Rumorosa, the majestic, forced you all to attention. The treacherous roads twisted through the mountain range and the narrow shoulder offered little hope to even a moment of inattention. Dizzy heights spilled down over the jagged cliff with Tijuana on the other side, then San Isidro, San Diego and Highway 5 onto Brentwood, an expanse of green, rolling hills.

That was the trip you'd known for years, the same trip once again as you crossed the border into Sonora. You and your sisters were sleepy from the drive, the familiar brown stretching for hours, lulling you to sleep as the sun sunk into the earth. Your father drove through the darkness while you nodded in and out of dreams. You woke when the car began to slow, opened your eyes to a hazy shape as a woman, unsteady in her steps, stumbled into the yellow glow of the car's headlights.

She calls out a deep, sad moan as you notice bloody clothes, tangled hair, streaks of red across her face. In that moment you know only the logic of dreams where bodies find form in restless wandering. Your sister asks, Where did she come from? Who is she? but still you don't believe what you see.

Your father tries to pull over, but your mother urges him on, remembering your uncle crossing those same mountains at night. He and his friends stopped to help the woman they'd found along the roadside, the one who vanished as they stepped out of the car while shadows slipped from under the bushes. Gradually shapes came into view, masked faces and arms extended into weapons strapped over their shoulders.

They forced your uncle and his friends into the mountains, stripped off their clothes and ordered them to dig their own graves. If not for a distraction, an owl in the trees or an animal rustling behind a rock, they wouldn't have had a chance. Your uncle and two of his friends escaped. The fourth they never found.

And so that night in the car with your family, your father drove on, never certain if the woman was left to die or to capture. Some days, even now, that haunting returns, disturbing your sleep so that some mornings you wake restless and wonder what would've happened if only?

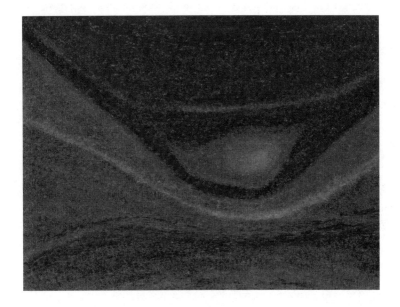

HUNGER

When your father was a boy, just six or seven years old, his job was to take the cattle and goats into the hills to feed. Every morning at sunrise he left for the hills hungry, hiking the three miles through the flatlands then further into the foothills, leading the herd to their feeding grounds, daydreaming all the while and wishing his quick feet could carry him away from the herd and far from the rumbling in his belly. When he reached the grazing grounds he'd wander in search of cherries hanging ripe or prickly tunas made all the sweeter by the sting in his hands, the thorns piercing through in his rush to reach the bright, pink centers. Some days the hunger was too much and he'd fall asleep in the grass or under a tree. One day while lying under a Sapote tree he dreamed of the fruit hanging beyond his reach, the expansive branches reaching to the sky taunting him. His long, restless sleep extended through the afternoon until the day dissolved into darkness and something startled him awake.

He struggled to his feet, wiping his eyes as daylight dissolved then rushed into the darkening night calling to the animals, fear spreading through his belly. He traveled down the winding path lined with Tejocote trees and gathered back into the herd the straying goats, their mournful cries breaking the stillness of the night. Beyond the path, a shifting shape under a tree caught his attention. Walking closer, he recognized the shape as a newborn goat, although not one from his herd. Perhaps a stray from someone passing before him, he thought. When he was just steps from the goat, the creature stood on all fours and grew larger as curled horns sprouted from its head.

The animal raced across the pasture, turning back to face your father with eyes glowing red just as it reached the fence separating the flatlands from the foothills. Your father remembered the stories of demons finding form in animals among the living. A haunting that grows stronger each time you hear the story no matter how far you've traveled since. The animal jumped the fence, turned back to look one last time, those red eyes now glowing words. You won't escape me burned into your father's memory so that he never again knew that countryside without fear.

PICKING MEMORIES

There's nothing better than fruit ripe from the tree, you think remembering the sticky juices running down your warm body and the burst of sweetness in your mouth. You remember the contests created with your sisters. She who picks the fastest, fills more buckets, works through the breaks wins without a prize. Each morning you're up by 5:00 and work until sunset, the blistering hours made bearable pretending it's no different than a pastime for those who pick for pleasure. You've seen them do the same without sweating, stopping before their baskets are full simply because they've had enough.

Your hands mark time in scars and scrapes. Your body remembers those long days in the fields when you could never pick enough to belie your father's hunger or free him from the memory of what it was to live without. And during those long days you also tried to forget so that even now memory transforms. When you tell the story what you remember most is your body in sticky sweetness, the taste of fruit still ripe on the tongue.

DEVIL

It was the beginning of summer, the start of heat and dry, dusty days when you first heard about the danger in the fields. You were sitting on the bed with your mother, watching as she folded laundry and the whole room, warm from the sun, was filled with outdoor smells. Hay and corn for tortillas, peach blossoms and sweet peas folded their scents into the clothes. Your mother worked methodically as she formed a sheet into squares smaller and smaller then tucked one end over the other before tossing it onto a pile. You laid your head against the dizzy sweetness, closed your eyes and tried to let the familiar smells comfort you.

But the afternoon air was too dry and the silence too long. Your sisters played quietly in the patio, obeyed your mother's warning to remain within her sight. You wanted to ask but didn't know what – you just knew that there was something churning deep down in your belly as if whatever was wrong on the outside had somehow settled there.

Your mother made your favorite lunch—chicken mole with rice and corn tortillas—but that day your hunger was different. It was more of a question, a need to know rumbling through your stomach. Finally you tried to ask but couldn't make the words fall into place and instead your hunger grew and spread through your body. You wanted to crawl into your mother's arms even though two babies now filled the space where you once fit.

Finally your mother began to speak. She told about the little girl taken from town in the night. Brothers and fathers searched with lights through the morning but found only a slip of fabric, a shred of her dress. A farmer discovered her body on his way to the hills as the sun brushed over the horizon, painting her shape. She lay naked, a slice through her side, spread out on a cactus like an offering. The devil's work, your mother told you. He lingered still, hiding behind trees or under rocks, waiting. That night your dreams were wild and running as you were chased breathless and woke into surrender. Every night after it was the same. During the day you imagined him lurking in the foothills, passing through town in disguise, changing shape into brother, father or uncle before you could recognize him.

Years later, you still try to understand. By now you've moved to a new country, grown into a different era where tragedy lies splayed across the daily pages. But still you never read those stories without remembering the ache of that day or the time before, when words hadn't yet captured your fear.

GREAT AUNT ROSA

Rosa grew up in a house of women. The one she knew as mother the others called Madam. To those on the outside the house was known for sin or for passion—the story changed depending on who you asked—but everyone knew that house with the men too mean and the lives too short. For Rosa the familiar defined her life. For years that house in the middle of town was home, the cantina in front, the rooms in back. Her sister, Eloisa, had other plans and left for a suitable house to call her own while Rosa stayed behind tending her mother's profession. There were so many wandering lonely or wounded, seldom was an empty evening.

Rosa grew into stories and learned to hold her attention like something fragile buried beneath mountain etched skies. She remembered each face and the shape of the lips spinning tales into the night. Her mother kept caged birds covered with vibrant feathers of yellow and blue. Cotorrito, a foul-mouthed parrot shared Rosa's room and translated her evenings. "Hi-jo de Pu-ta," echoed through the house each morning.

One man she remembered with longing. He distorted her dreams and clung to her body long after he'd left. He said he'd take care of her. As if offering a favor, said he'd erase her history with his name.

Rosa stayed and made her life there among the women. She never regretted the life she passed up. Like her sister, she simply desired her own.

DISTURBANCES

Whispers carried on a baby's cry. Lungs filled with the first needy breaths, hungry for more. These are the babies born beyond love, the babies whose lives are sealed before they arrive. Their mothers haven't the time or the means to feed them, learn instead to stifle them swiftly and try to forget. The tiny bodies lie stiff in shallow graves of clay soil behind the house on the outskirts of town where men pay women for pleasure.

Close to the garden lie the deeper graves, the men carved open with knives. Scarred flesh and tattoos give them away. These are the men nobody misses, the ones who are too mean, too angry. It's always a matter of time until they're lost among the unloved. Murdered in the night over the attention of a woman, leaving with "puta" ripe on the tongue.

Years from now, when this house has changed its story nobody will want to live here. People will walk by and feel its restlessness, the sadness of lives too short, the abruptness in passing.

They'll hear a chorus of voices through the silence, feel a chill across the flesh no matter how many coats of paint or new walls. Flowers in the garden take root alongside brittle bones. Major disturbances have a way of forcing themselves back up to the surface.

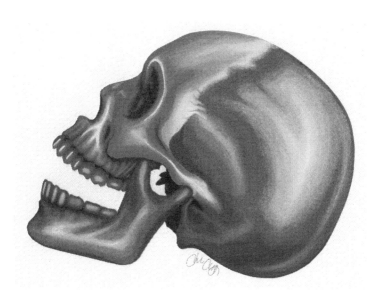

THE THINGS THEY SELL

At the baby casket store they sell all the sorrow you need as you trek over cobblestone paths where diesel fume alleys leak visible air and sweat drips down your arms and legs, gritty from the journey. Mornings you walk past the storefront displaying tiny white caskets and each time the weight like a dirge knocks through your skull. You hear the tone and lilt of the sentences without words, the paragraphs searching for story.

At the cantina the women's faces make you think of the game la Loteria. Pictures of la sirena, la chalupa, la dama call to you. You cover their images with cheap trinkets and hold back your voice, your memory like the wisps of smoke from painted lips. You follow with your eyes, those thin streams intermingling and forming bursts of clouds over talking heads.

Between guayaba trees you chase white ghosts, shake free sweet fruit and cut loose the bruise. In a glimpse a piece of memory holds then lifts with the screech of an owl, the rush of wings breaking through sky. Across the dusty street, the dulceria beckons with tres leches cakes and marzipan. You venture inside, brush your fingers over granules of sugar-coated skulls and imagine the taste of death dissolving on your tongue.

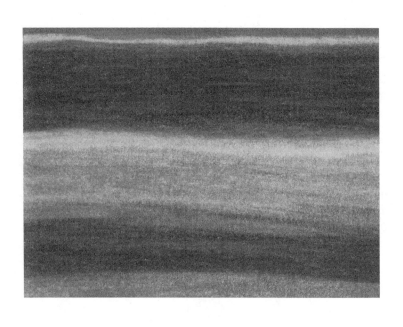

SPIRIT

It was December, before the Posadas began, but already the excitement spread through the streets in colorful cordeles, decorations for la virgen. Your dreams were piñatas spilling tamarind candies and fruits, bright costumes and firecrackers bursting open the night.

Before bed you and your friends invented games, ran through the streets weaving between groups of neighbors returning from the plaza. Not far from your home was where your friend Ana lived, the old house split down the middle by a lonely corridor emptying into a patio with a stone well. A tin bucket swayed from a rope, a relic from the family before.

One night as you and Ana played in front of her house, you saw a burst of white light just before the streets fell into darkness. You stood in the pitch-black night, shrieking and laughing, searching the sky for the moon. A voice across the street, Ana's mother, beckoned you both inside.

The two of you entered the dark house in careful steps. Your soft laughter spilled down the corridor and echoed off the walls. You saw it first, the dim light outlining the body giving shape to her form. As your eyes adjusted you saw the woman standing next to the well. She wore a long skirt. A rebozo spilled down her head as she peered into the water. You stood still and watched, searching for sense as your laughter dissolved to fear. She was nobody you knew. Your screams blended with Ana's, shooting a piercing shriek through the woman.

Ana's mother caught you both against her body as you stumbled for the door. Within minutes the lights were back on, the spot at the well empty. She's looking for her son, Ana's mother explained when Ana told her what you'd seen. It was her youngest boy who drowned there, she'd said pointing toward the well. And now her spirit can't rest.

You felt your skin tingle at the thought, a cold shiver pass through your body. What could be worse? You imagined the endless search, forever reliving a single moment until it replaces all memory.

EL DIA DE SAN JUAN

It's San Juan who keeps us safe, Rosa's story began. During the Revolution the Zapatistas called on him for protection, knelt before his image and prayed. You imagined grown men humbled by the three-foot statue dressed in a brown frock, lasso swinging loosely at his waist and small sandals painted onto his feet.

He gave them courage. Rosa leaned close and you knew she believed by her narrowing eyes. Looking skyward without focus, she squinted into the past and pulled history from legend.

The Zapatistas hid in the mountains and watched clouds of red dust spin from the earth as soldiers on horseback raced across the hilltop then pulled tight on the reigns just as they reached the edge of the cliff. Looking down, the soldiers saw the arc of sun rising into the sky reflected in a blue-green lake where they remembered rocky soil. The soldiers circled the lake, pulled maps from their satchels and sought to explain.

San Juan did his work, Rosa said, her voice deep, eyes clenched tight. You watched wrinkles ripple across her forehead and lines form around her mouth as she sculpted words into stories. He changed land into water and kept our men safe.

The words of the Commander rolled from Rosa's lips. Bring me the statue, he ordered his men, sending them into town. By stealing San Juan's image the Commander thought he'd claim its strength for himself, but the statue wouldn't be taken. Opening the church doors the next morning, the priest saw miniature footprints leading the way up the steps and down a path to the altar where the statue stood with water dripping from his frock, tiny, muddy sandals covering his feet.

The people named him patron saint of their town, kept him guarded under lock and key and cast a replica for everyday glances. Once a year he's honored in celebration, his statue displayed as worshippers grow weak in the knees and faint at the sight, their bodies remembering a moment when earth and faith collided. You wish you could climb into the safety of Rosa's words, into that time before, strengthened by San Juan's powers and the protection belief provided.

BATTLING ELOISA

As soon as she learned to walk, Rosa told you, Eloisa was already leaving. She wandered from home at sunrise shrouded in hazy orange, passing mornings on grassy slopes wet with mountain air. Afternoons melted on warm cobblestones as evening's colors faded to yellow gray. Each day she was guided by the map etched in her mind, men wanting to take before she could give. Her mother and sister might be lost to that house, but she knew no rooms would contain her.

As youngest sister, Eloisa learned from the others – carried their history in her body, a chill in her blood. But she thought beyond her body when seeking a future of her own. Barely thirteen, Eloisa agreed when a new life was offered, accepting a husband long past her age with children in mind. Some called her new life respectable business, but for Eloisa it was the choice that mattered most. Through her days she stitched fabrics fashioned to clothes carried down dusty roads for profit. Each year a new baby filled her arms, so many needs, so quick to grow.

Eloisa made her own way and kept her distance from those who questioned. With a gun under her bed and a switchblade between her breasts she created a world safe for those she called her own.

Eloisa mastered her own rules, shot open the sky when passion found her at last. The men came to serenade her daughters and fight her sons, but they faced Eloisa instead. Rosa swore it was more than maternal for Eloisa. Not just a mother's warning. For Eloisa there was pleasure in the fight. Her survival depended on it, was as natural as breath.

FLAMES

In the kitchen Eloisa made tamales with your other aunts while you and your sisters played with cousins, enchanted by sweet cinnamon rising on steam. Outside the window deep voices spilled stories. You heard a shot of laughter, something about a failed business venture, another's dream searching for gold.

On hands and knees you and your cousins crawled beneath the table, fumbled to the other side, then chased each other around cabinet and chair. Breathless and laughing you stood still for a moment and closed your eyes, savoring the smells of dough wrapped in corn husks and listening to the murmur of voices, safely distanced from that other world of making money, keeping house.

While your Aunts cooked, the lights dimmed then faded to dark. You heard her footsteps crossing the room, saw Eloisa's shadow against the window as the drawer screeched open and she fumbled for candles. You looked through the darkness just then, all of you looking—sisters, cousins, aunts, the men. There might've been a voice but none heard it, only the silence contained in that moment as the flame exploded into the corral and leapt through the trees.

You thought a ghost before you heard the scream throughout your body, burning your throat, filling your mouth. You scrambled to the bedroom, racing cousins and sisters. You pulled at arms and legs, each one trying to hold another back, each one trying to be the first to the door while behind you the men laughed at your fear.

When the light returned, Eloisa coaxed you all back to the kitchen. You took your place at the table, too scared to eat.

It's a good omen, your uncle laughed, reminding you of the stories, of gold revealed in flame. But that night your dreams were dancing figures circling rings of fire. Faces with sallow cheeks peered through blackened eyes, thin bodies and long arms reaching out.

The next day your father and uncles carried shovels to the corral. They dug for hours, but you weren't thinking about money. The men hardly listened when you tried to tell them what you'd seen in dreams, concerned only with the work at hand and all it might afford.

SEARCHING

It was your abuelo who first saw fire dancing through the limbs of cherry trees. He was still a young man learning to work the soil, breaking into dusty earth. He glanced upward, felt sweat trickle over his dirty cheeks, closed his eyes for a moment then opened them to hot orange flames shooting from the ground. Two uniformed men stood at attention looking beyond your abuelo toward the mountains. He followed their gaze but saw only the space where they'd been when he turned back to face them. Remembering the stories of hidden treasures, he walked closer to where they'd stood and discovered the cave. Inside was a wooden chest, musky and thick, its lock jammed tight.

That's when your abuelo remembered the old Zapatista General, Rosa tells you. Everyone knew about him back then. The old man was famous for his treasures. His pockets full from all that he'd gathered during the revolution.

Some said he'd taken from – others claimed he took back – but everyone knew golden handfuls of coins had spilled from the General's pockets into a deep wooden chest he carried into the mountains, searching for a cave to conceal his fortune. He left two of his men to stand guard. At night, a curandera appeared and cast a spell to keep their secret safe.

When the old man returned, he found only remains, coats, hats and scattered bones—his guards long ago murdered by enemy soldiers. There he remained searching day after day, his treasures lost to chants and incantations. The cave, dissolved on the curandera's words, reappears a single day each year. Only the curandera knows when and only those like your abuelo, who stumbled upon it, know of the truths buried in legend. When your abuelo remembered the old general, he raced home with scattered thoughts searching for form. Breathless, he stood in the doorway until his frantic words burst open the story and spread through town.

The next day the townspeople followed your abuelo up the winding, mountain road, some on horseback to help with the load, but when they arrived at the spot only cherry trees stood where the cave had been. But no one ever doubted, Rosa tells you, and no one ever forgot that day because we were all part of something then. It was something we could believe in, something to hope for.

You hear past and present blending in Rosa's voice and wish you could feel the excitement for yourself, wish for a time when anything was possible and you never once questioned faith.

PASSING LEGENDS

Over marshy green water trees bend their limbs, cascading twigs skim the surface like slender fingers. Solid roots stretch arteries over caked soil, branch out and plunge below the water's surface into firm calves, thick thighs, unyielding.

On the shore, men tip bottles to their cracked lips, swallow hard, swap stories. Calloused fingers fumble over taught guitar strings, deep voices wrap around a melody and nobody remembers the words.

As the sun drops, they toss their bottles aside, dive through murky ripples, feet slapping against the surface. Gathering air into expanded lungs, one dips under and swims toward the trees, dizzy from drink. He doesn't notice or care about the long legs reaching out, doesn't notice or care until they twist around his body, hold him tight against the struggle. His shouts swallowed in water, he gives life to the legend. She'd slithered from serpent to woman into murky deep green, gradually becoming part of the lake. She seduced and tricked him into one final dance as she pulled his last breath away.

CAMECUARO ROOTS

Near the path women roll balls of flour and water, mold them into tortillas then stand over pans of sizzling oil watching tostadas take shape. Along the shore the men sell miniature fishnets, resplendent in rainbow hues. The children, drawn by color, imagine possibility. In shallow water they stand next to trees with sunken roots, their nets chasing quick, silver flashes.

At the end of the lake the cousins and tios swim in fresh water pools. One stands back, scans the surface and tells you he'll never forget. It's not safe he warns, for men or drunks. There was a time when everyone knew. A serpent, he claimed, led them astray some even seeing her form.

Back then the men met without families under the shade of sheltering trees. Bottles raised in a toast, they shared stories and jokes before diving through cloudy ripples, never noticing the tree roots gripping the soil, sliding a long arm down the side of the bank. Always too late, the others discovered one missing from the group. Hidden limbs pulled him down, they claimed, trapping him in strong thighs, powerful arms. They've cleaned up the lake, your tio says, but some things you just can't trust. You stand and listen, wait and watch his face slowly reveal his fears.

ROSA AFTER NOON

       Every afternoon Rosa sat in front of her store with needle and thread while the women and niños gathered. The little ones collected candies, marzapan and cabesitas, while Rosa swapped stories with the women. Together they stitched their way through dusty afternoons as the sun descended toward evening. Behind them the parrot Cotorrito swung in his cage while the niños waited eagerly for his words. The women never spoke of Rosa's other life, but Cotorrito held the memory, cussing at the niños, *Chinga tu madre cabron!*

       Crazy bird, Rosa laughed, thinking of the stories he could tell. The women tilted their heads and pretended not to care about the stories Rosa refused to share. The niños gathered at the steps and waited for more of the forbidden words to spill their way.

       Rosa was mystery to the niños, a question for the women, tales men told one another at night. But she never forgot who she'd been, just kept that a separate story.

HERMINIA SHOT BOTH WAYS

The day Herminia was shot, nobody noticed revolutionaries arriving from the road of the twin ranches or the soldiers entering from the opposite side of town. Nobody was looking, nobody saw. Herminia was crouching in a doorway when a bullet nicked her shoulder, a red flower spreading through her blouse. It was during the revolution, when women and girls knew their place in attics and secret rooms while guards stood watch over roads and entryways.

Herminia, tired of hiding and thinking the end of the fighting was near, stepped onto the cobbled street leading to the plaza and swallowed breaths of fresh, mountain air. The others soon met her, women and girls cooped up too long gathered in the streets. The days had grown calm, the guards granted leave.

Buenos dias, como amanecio? The women's voices spread through the streets, broke open the stillness and filled the air. They gathered at the plaza, as they'd done before the fighting began, took back their Sundays and shared stories and plans.

The day Herminia was shot nobody heard the soldiers branching out, slipping into the alleys. Nobody felt the streets pulsing with the revolutionaries' march. The women heard only their voices and laughter rising and were so captivated they never bothered to wonder if it would last.

In the center of town, on the edge of the plaza, the two troops met in bullets. Blasts of gunshot and the women's screams shattered the calm. The women ran for cover, tried to push through doors and break open windows. Herminia saw bits and parts—an arm lifted, a hand covering lips, flowing dark hair. She felt her hands pound against doors, felt screams lift from her chest, her body falling. She pulled herself inward, lay huddled in a doorway when the bullet cut through her shoulder.

Herminia never remembered the truth after that, whether another bullet grazed the other side, leaving her marked by both troops or if it was just her mind playing tricks – something she'd first constructed in fear then clung to so she wouldn't be forgotten. It was the story she told over and over as she settled into the years. By then she'd learned how quickly a lifetime can pass.

SAN ISIDRO

You remember the day in flowers, the countryside in picnics. San Isidro, the patron of farmers honored in avas and guayavas, cherries and cañas. The month of May in calabasitas, the tender, ripe zucchini harvested for celebration. The day begins in the streets as farmers lead the bulls and you scatter flowers from your mother's garden, following the procession to the plaza for mass.

In the afternoon, you and your sisters climb on a wagon and ride to the countryside, jumping off to collect fruit and flowers along the way. Your mother points out the sneezing flower as you pick your way along the path, then back on the wagon she shows you how to squeeze just right, the blossom held between finger and thumb. Inhale slowly, breaths released in sudden bursts, mouth wide open, your nose a prickly fire. Your mother feeds you names, points out the medicinal plants identified in leaf and flower while you jump back down into the road's dizzy curves, reaching for the yellow petals.

In the meadow your father lights a fire while you and your sisters search for cañas, each of you trying to find hidden riches in the thickest stalks. You know the day by the angle of the sun, never wonder at beginnings or endings the way you remember it now.

You return at sundown to a ritual in water, young women and girls run through the streets while mothers and fathers, brothers and friends shower you in brimming buckets, a wish for luck. You remember the excitement washed in possibility, envisioned yourself lucky. It was enough, the sweet corn cañas, your fingers painted in cherry stains and the scents of flowers, the power in what the earth yielded, your body's own mystery. You lived like that then, in a world of awe and wonder, never questioning, how long will it last?

LAB COATS

Earlier that morning you followed your sisters to the end of the road, wishing you were old enough to continue along the path into the schoolyard. Instead, they sent you back toward home where already your mother's chores had begun. You stayed out of her way all morning, then reappeared as her voice called to you, as if led on an invisible thread.

It was Wednesday, you knew, because that was the day you carried the wicker basket in the plaza market as your mother passed her hands over ripening fruit, inspected for bumps and bruises hinting at decay. As you followed your mother through the plaza, the hot air hung over you, motionless. The market, usually filled with mothers bargaining, small children weaving between their legs, was nearly empty, the afternoon washed in silence. Your mother grabbed your hand and led you to the presidencia at the center of the plaza. The voice from the steps warned mothers to take their children home and find a hiding place. Not sent by the government, you heard. Dressed in lab coats to look like doctors. Not who they seem to be.

Your mother pulled you by the arm. Together you ran toward the school, took the path all the way through, but it happened so quickly you didn't have time to understand and then your sisters were footsteps running behind you until you were breathless and you heard your mother's voice sharp like anger. Inside the house you ran for the bedroom, but her voice startled you to stop. Your mother dragged a ladder from behind the stairs and leaned it against the wall. You climbed up, two sisters in front, three in back, the trap door a narrow slice in the ceiling. As your oldest sister pulled in the ladder, "Keep the door shut" was the last you heard.

You were hot and thirsty, too scared to complain, crouched beneath the attic beams, the street silence wrong, you there with your sisters, the little one crying. Sitting so still you heard every creak of the house, never knew time so slow. As you drifted to sleep, a gun cracked open the night, your heart a frantic burst inside your chest. That'll keep them away, you heard Eloisa say, relieved the voice was hers. She led you and your sisters down from the attic on the calm of her voice, her promises lulling, They'll stay away, They'll stay away. Your whole family slept on mattresses in the kitchen that night, but you never closed your eyes, knowing already how little it took to disappear.

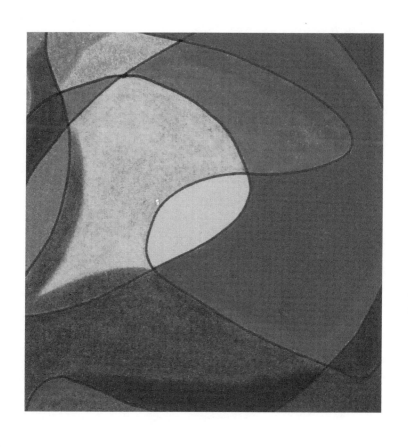

TIN MARIN

De tin marin
de don Pingue
cucara, macara
titere fue!
"Titere fue, you're it!"

When your cousins visited, you slept in the front bedroom,
all of the girls packed tight in two beds, daring and double daring each
other into the corral alone at night. In the farthest corner along the adobe
wall, behind the avocado trees, an old brick marked the spot. You'd seen
shadows and movement, felt the hand against the nape of your neck, one
bony finger sliding down. You were never alone then. Each of you met
the devil in dreams, had your own version. Hazy red taking shape or the
wooden handle of an axe.

Each of you tried to be the bravest but none made it beyond the
first tree. You'd hold your breath, fingers clenched, and scream when you
heard the rustling near the wall. Wind or stray papers dancing from last
night's bonfire, spirited souls or someone playing tricks. Running back,
your body light as if drifting, your bare feet slapped against cold dirt until
you reached the patio where the other girls waited in a huddle. The ghosts
only found form when you were alone. Avoiding solitude seemed the
obvious solution.

Sometimes still there's a lingering memory as if something lost,
a phantom pain. Together you learned to conquer fear. You never forgot
the weightlessness of yourself in terror and the force of you as one.

INDEPENDENCE DAY

You remember Mexican independence crafted in miniature hot air balloons, the work of boys. Small hands pattern tissue paper, wood sticks and glue. An aluminum cup holds the cloth as gasoline seeps through. At sunset they release them, illuminated bubbles suspended and drifting, then chase through the streets as if after dreams. Front doors of houses propped open lead into patios, spill out to corrals. Catching the breath of boys, the cups scrape across soil and grass. Fathers scoop up and re-release them in a flash of light, send the boys scrambling over stone walls and other obstacles in the night.

You stand in the street, a small girl watching balloons in parrot colors flicker across a dark-purple sky. It's their night, fathers and sons, but still you imagine yourself in buoyancy. Weightless and volatile, you wonder where you'd land

DAILY CONCERNS

You climb onto her lap and rest into softness drifting like slumber. She's not like your mother, closer to sister, married to Jesus, how much he demands. Much less than a husband, she tells you and that's all you hear.

Smooth rosary beads slip through her fingers. Mary's medallion, a cool blue shimmer skims over your skin. One day, she says, you may hear them, voices demanding or quivering cries. Then what matters you'll know in your body.

How will I know? you wonder, the beads passing now through your hands. If this is the end of desire or only where it begins?

VIRGEN DE GUADALUPE

You wake to song and orange-red strokes across the sky, the air redolent with pine needles. A hand-strewn path welcomes La Virgen and Juan Diego's memory. Your day begins in colors as you decorate doorways, stretch across streets cordeles in green, white and red. Baskets swollen with flowers and food—tamales, guayavas, zapotes, calabasa cosida y chayotes carried in offering. Dressed in native clothes you try to connect this history with who you've become.

Bells ring in the plaza. You follow in response, guided to mass in tradition and the body's memory of what it was to know faith. You sit silent through blessings, make the signs, tolerate forgiveness. Back outside food and offerings spread through the plaza. Together you break bread, share until the baskets are empty and you wonder, What's left?

Changing from native to Mestiza you return for a second celebration, to a night of searing bright light. El torito flares as someone grabs the bull-head and charges, the horns a hot blue fire. Later they burn the Castillo. The remains of the bamboo castle cascade in points of light, La Virgen's crown shoots into the sky as grand finale, warping memory while you stand aside watching just outside of time.

DANCE OF OLD MEN

Grey-bearded men bend onto canes. With faces masked in brown creases and heels rapid tap-tapping, the bodies still limber betray. Dancing into age they've nothing to fear, these young men disguised as old.

Tia Rosa? you asked the first time you saw them dance their way across the stage. *How do they dance without growing tired when outside their bodies are old?*

Mija, she smiled, *It's a game, don't you see?* and her eyes wandered off toward the sky. *Mija*, she repeated, *we should be like those men, our bodies altered in play.*

You clung to their movements timed in unison, stood mesmerized by each tap of the cane. You wondered what stories they knew, listened for words in the dance, and watched for a slip of the truth.

You'd believed them back then, the age and the ease and the wisdom they wore in their faces. A good trick you think as you've grown through the years, memories fading and altered by time.

ROSA REMEMBERED

Even then you knew Rosa had another life, understood your way through the silences and what was left unsaid. What you didn't know was the exact shape of the story. You understood the urgency of forgetting, molding memory and history to a more suitable form, a dress she could wear, a size that fit.

In Rosa's store, the bar and stools remain. Sweets are displayed on the bottom shelves, canned goods replace beer bottles, the mirror reflects a gathering of women and no one speaks of the rooms in back. You imagined her leaving, as if beginnings require departure, imagined a journey and introductions, a great distance between what had been and what came next, and all along there she was, her life changing shape among the familiar.

YELLOW

You remember Eloisa in yellow. The color of flowers along the road, canned juice you buy in the States, your mother's dress on Sunday, lined paper ruled with margins where you scratch English words in tiny print, coveted stars you'll never earn for perfect attendance. Yellow the color of landscape half-way to Mexico, stepping over borders, defining a home. Yellow in loneliness, the friends you leave behind each time crossing over. Yellow in tejocotes blushing red, peaches ripe against the skin, picking your way through the seasons. Yellow the color of sickness and disease, the ones who never leave their beds, the stories the tias tell. Yellow the color of Eloisa's eyes like nothing you'd seen before, as if all the flowers were reflected there or the stars a fierce glow while the English words seek form, long to give shape to the space where she lay. Yellow the color of Eloisa dying. Eloisa who left, who like you wanted a different life and found a way. Eloisa lost in story, those yellow eyes all you see.

WITNESS

Music spreads over rooftops in Tequila toasts, rain on adobe, touch to taste. Morning shower in firewood drifts on gray clouds. Silence slides beneath guitars as distant voices transform memory to song and we strain for the words. We'll remember tortillas wrapped in brown paper, milk emptied in buckets, skimming fat off the surface, sweet restraint. Scorpions hidden under teja cover falling into a scamper. The roadside in stray dogs, red dirt pressed to mud filtered into scent.

On the rooftop our arms briefly touch as we pass the bottle between us. Fire in the throat soothed by cool lemon. The afternoon sky a blanket of clouds pressing down the heat. Resting against teja cover, we listen to the echo of mariachi horns drifting from the plaza. The narrow road stretching beneath us holds the memory of wagon and cart, the groove of wheels worn into stone. Its twists and curves lead to the center of town where the band strikes notes to the voice of song.

The cars from the States don't fit on these roads, take up too much space in the drive. Tomorrow we'll ride away from the center, back down narrow alleys and dirt paths, find our way by the shape of mountains. Cradled in hills we'll pass the outlines of faces and formations, craggy woman bent, gemstone eyes, still searching for home.

ACKNOWLEDGEMENTS

We would like to thank our family members, in no particular order, for supporting our creativity. Our mothers Carolina Cortez and Linda Eppley, fathers Samuel Eppley and Ramiro Cortez, sisters and sister-in-law Juana Padilla, Maria Elena Ordaz, Raquel Madrigal, Martha Hurtado, Rocio Dominguez, Isabel Calderon, Catalina Prado, Carolina Estrada, Rochelle Melander, and brother, Harold Eppley. Thanks also to Irene Barnard, Cedric Brown, Carol Feiner, Jo Ginsberg, Barbara Leff, Nina Schuyler, and Cassie Tunick for reading various drafts and providing valuable feedback.

MARIA DEL CARMEN CORTEZ & REBEKAH EPPLEY
are a married couple living in Oakland. Rebekah is a librarian
at Oakland Public Library. Carmen is a Permaculturalist and a
student of herbal medicine at Ohlone Herbal College.